Weekly Reader Children's Book Club presents

Two Is Company

Story by Judy Delton

Pictures by Giulio Maestro

Crown Publishers, Inc.   New York

Weekly Reader Children's Book Club Edition

The text of this book is set in 18/30 Rector.
The illustrations are pencil drawings reproduced in three colors.
Designed by Giulio Maestro.
Library of Congress Catalog Card Number: 75-45180
ISBN 0-517-526018

To Elaine Knox-Wagner
   for all the houses we've built together

Bear and Duck were two good friends.
Duck was Bear's best friend.
One day Duck hurried to Bear's house.
"Bear! Bear!" he said, knocking on the
door. "We have a new neighbor!
Chipmunk has moved in down the path!"
"Oh," said Bear.
"Yes," said Duck. "Chipmunk bought
Groundhog's house."
"How nice," said Bear.

"And I am having a party for Chipmunk
this afternoon," said Duck. "Be at my
house at three o'clock. Okay?"

"But, Duck," said Bear, "we always pick
blackberries at three o'clock!"

"We can pick blackberries another
time, Bear."

"They will be overripe, Duck. They won't taste good then!"

"One more day won't matter, Bear. We can go tomorrow."

"Ah, Duck," said Bear, "Chipmunk is probably too busy for a party. Moving in is always hard work."

"No," said Duck. "Chipmunk is all settled. I helped her hang her curtains this morning."

Bear shook his head.

"I don't know, Duck. If it was *me*, I would not want a party. All that fuss would embarrass me. Besides, Chipmunk may be shy. Have you thought of that, Duck?"

"Chipmunk is not shy," said Duck. "She *wants* to meet her new neighbors. I have to go now. I have to invite the others. See you at three o'clock."

Bear sat down in his rocking chair.
"Maybe the others can't come," thought
Bear. "Maybe they will be busy."
Bear rocked in his chair.
Before long it was three o'clock.
Squirrel passed Bear's house.
Squirrel waved.
"Are you coming, Bear?" he asked.
"I'll be along," said Bear. "You go
on ahead."

Bear got ready slowly. First he washed the dishes. Then he polished his shoes. Then he ironed his vest. Finally he put on his tie and started down the path.

He looked at the trees; he talked to
the birds; but at last he reached
Duck's house. He knocked on the door.

"Bear," whispered Duck. "You are late.
Come in. Here is your party hat."
Bear put on his hat.

Everyone was singing and playing games.
Balloons and streamers were everywhere.

Bear sat down on the couch.

Chipmunk sat next to him.

"Hello, Bear," said Chipmunk. "I have
been looking forward to meeting you."

"Hello, Chipmunk," said Bear, taking
some salted peanuts, "too bad about
your house."

"What about my house?" asked Chipmunk.

"The water," said Bear, sadly shaking
his head. "That is why Groundhog moved.
He was flooded out, poor thing...."

"It is nice and dry now," said Chipmunk.

"Wait until spring, Chipmunk. You'll be
moving out when the snow melts."

"Dear me! I hope not," said Chipmunk.

Just then Duck clapped his wings.

"It is time for Chipmunk to open her presents."

Everyone gathered around Chipmunk.

There was a dust mop from Duck.

There was a teapot from Squirrel,
and Rabbit brought a chocolate cake.

Bear had not brought anything.
Everyone stared at Bear.
"I—er—didn't have time to shop," said
Bear as he stared at his feet.
"Let's all have a piece of Rabbit's
chocolate cake," said Chipmunk quickly.

Rabbit cut the cake and passed a slice
to everyone.

"I have my own cake at home," said Bear.

"Have a piece anyway," said Rabbit.

"No," said Bear, looking at his pocket
watch. "It is time for me to leave.
I have to weed my garden."

Bear went to find Duck.

Duck and Chipmunk were standing
in a corner.

"I have to leave, Duck," said Bear. "I
have to weed my garden."

"Okay," said Duck, "we will see you
tomorrow."

"Who's we?" asked Bear.

"Chipmunk and myself," said Duck. "I
thought we could show her where the
berry patch is."

"I am looking forward to it," said
Chipmunk.

Bear leaned over.

"Duck," he whispered, "that is *our* secret berry patch."

"There are enough berries for all of us," said Duck. "We will meet at Three Pines at three o'clock."

"I'll be there," said Chipmunk.

Bear was angry. He kicked stones all
the way home.

The next afternoon, Bear and Duck
met at Three Pines. They sat on a
stump and waited for Chipmunk.
"Chipmunk is late," said Bear, looking
at his watch. "You said three o'clock.
I could be home weeding my garden."
"I hope Chipmunk isn't lost," said Duck.
"I like to be on time," said Bear. "You
are always on time, Duck. That is
important with friends."
"Bear, you are often late yourself.
Chipmunk may be sick. Dear me, I
should have called her."
"It is three thirty, Duck. Your friend
is half an hour late. We should have
gone by ourselves."

"Here she comes!" shouted Duck.
Chipmunk was running.
"I'm sorry to be late," she said. "I
didn't notice the time."
"No hurry," said Duck. "I'm glad you
didn't get lost."
"I could have finished weeding my
garden," muttered Bear.
"Oh, dear," said Chipmunk. "I forgot
to bring a pail!"
Bear groaned.

"Bear has two pails," said Duck. "He will be glad to share."

The three walked to the blackberry patch. They all began to pick berries. In an hour Bear and Duck had filled their pails.

Chipmunk's pail had only a few berries
in it.

Bear yawned.

Then he stretched out under a tree.

"It's warm in this hot sun," he
complained.

"I seem to be slow at this," said Chipmunk sadly. "The blackberry bushes are a bit high for me."

"That is all right, Chipmunk," said Duck. "You are new at berry picking. Let me help."

Duck helped Chipmunk fill the pail and then the three set off for home.

"Good-bye, Chipmunk," said Duck. "We
will see you Friday morning at the fair!"
"Fine!" said Chipmunk, waving a paw.
Bear and Duck walked on together.

"Chipmunk is nice," said Duck.

Bear didn't say anything.

"What is bothering you, Bear?"

"Nothing," said Bear.

"Don't lie, Bear. I know something is
bothering you."

"Why does Chipmunk have to come
everywhere with us?" grumbled Bear.

"Now she is even coming to the fair. And the seats on the Ferris wheel only have room for two. Someone will have to sit alone. Some things are better with two," Bear said.

"We can all fit in one seat, Bear."

"It will be too tight, Duck."

"But, Bear, Chipmunk is small. We can all fit."

"I don't care," said Bear. "Chipmunk is late and forgetful. And she takes forever picking berries."

"The blackberry bushes are too high for her," said Duck. "And she needs friends, Bear."

The two came to Bear's house.

"Well, I don't need any more friends,"
grumbled Bear as he went in and
slammed the door.
Bear grumbled as he got supper.
"Chipmunk, Chipmunk, Chipmunk!
Nothing is the same since she moved in."
Bear grumbled as he ate supper and
as he washed the dishes. Then he
remembered his weeding.

He grumbled as he walked toward his
garden with his hoe. When Bear reached
his garden, he stopped. Half of his
garden was weeded. "How did that
happen?" said Bear.

Bear thought and thought.

"Of course," said Bear.

Bear put down his hoe and went
into the house.

He picked up the telephone and called
Duck. But Duck said, "No, Bear, I did not
weed your garden. I have been making
blackberry jelly. I have to go now.
My jelly is on the stove. Good-bye, Bear."
"Good-bye, Duck," said Bear.
The next day Bear went to market.
He met Rabbit at the carrot counter.

"Rabbit," said Bear, "thank you for weeding my garden!"

"I didn't weed your garden," said Rabbit. "I have been busy canning carrots for the winter."

"Oh," said Bear, rubbing his head thoughtfully.

Bear paid for his flour and eggs and started home.

When he was almost there, he saw his
tomatoes moving. Bear walked faster.
"Chipmunk!" cried Bear. "What are
you doing?"

"Weeding your garden. Weeding is easy
for me because I am so short and close
to the ground."

"Why—er—thank you, Chipmunk," said
Bear. "That is very kind of you."

"You're welcome, Bear," said Chipmunk.

"Would you like a glass of lemonade?"
asked Bear.
"That would be lovely," said Chipmunk.
Chipmunk and Bear each drank a glass of
lemonade. Then Chipmunk left for home.

Soon Bear's telephone rang.

"Hello, Bear!" said Duck. "I've—ah—
been thinking it over. About the fair—
perhaps you and I should go alone."

"No," said Bear. "I think Chipmunk
should come. She will be lonely."

"But, Bear, I thought you said…"

"Look, Duck," said Bear. "I changed my
mind. Can't I change my mind?"